T0156413

Twisted Peace
Colors Hidden in Shadow

PLUS THE FIRST SIX CHAPTERS OF CAIN THE
FIRST DROP

DENNIS BEGGS

authorHOUSE®

AuthorHouse™
1663 Liberty Drive
Bloomington, IN 47403
www.authorhouse.com
Phone: 1-800-839-8640

© 2011 Dennis Beggs. All rights reserved.

No part of this book may be reproduced, stored in a retrieval system, or transmitted by any means without the written permission of the author.

First published by AuthorHouse   5/31/2011

ISBN: 978-1-4634-1570-9 (e)
ISBN: 978-1-4567-6073-1 (dj)
ISBN: 978-1-4567-6074-8 (sc)

Library of Congress Control Number: 2011905214

Printed in the United States of America

Any people depicted in stock imagery provided by Thinkstock are models, and such images are being used for illustrative purposes only. Certain stock imagery © Thinkstock.

This book is printed on acid-free paper.

Because of the dynamic nature of the Internet, any web addresses or links contained in this book may have changed since publication and may no longer be valid. The views expressed in this work are solely those of the author and do not necessarily reflect the views of the publisher, and the publisher hereby disclaims any responsibility for them.

People throughout time have written of beauty and happiness, focusing on the vibrant colors of the world. Although it is nice to be drawn away from the dark shadows of reality, this focus denies us the other side of the world. When we focus our eyes away from the darkness of the soul, we are unaware that without depression, happiness would be unknown and unneeded.

As people, we are not always happy, yet depression is looked upon as a sickness. I have seen both sides. Let me ask you: is it the depressed who are sick, or is it the part of society that wakes up every morning putting on their fake smiles? They give their advice to the world, the same advice that they themselves do not take. They figure that if they preach it enough, it will miraculously turn true for them.

We all know life is hard. Deal with it as you see fit. Let the hypocrites feed themselves on their lies; soon they, too, will focus upon the shadow instead of hiding from the dark.

Adapting

You think you know your life, especially how you personally feel. Yet through some mystical force, you can't get it right. You have constant fears of being misunderstood. You try hard to make a good life, yet always fall short, hurting the ones you love. All the time, you honestly feel that you're a good person. To adapt to another person is hard; the blending of two emotional souls is a touchy thing. You feel that you're being considerate, doing the best you can, while constantly learning and adjusting to this other being. Yet when you know you're doing one thing, the other person feels differently. Regardless of what you think, the feelings of the other are all there is. This plays on both sides, and pleasing the other seems almost impossible. The truth is that pleasing one another is possible through the trials and failures of life, and the desire on both sides to adapt to the other.

All in a moment

All in a moment, everything can change. You take your life for granted when you look at the clock, planning your next hour. There is no guarantee you will see another morning come. Each breath does not ensure the next. Do you spend all your time planning for a future you may never see? Can you not see that anticipating the sunset takes the beauty from the pending sunrise? Leave your troubles behind; that's where they are anyway, in the past. Enjoy today, because you are lucky to have it.

If you read the paper or watch the news, you see that many will not have the chance you do now. Have you ever heard the phrase, "I didn't think it would happen to me"? Chances are, it will be you one day. When it is and you're on the news, there will be someone watching your story—and the cycle goes on.

Look at the facts. All the people who died yesterday were planning to wake up today, just like you now. Even while reading this, your mind is subconsciously planning your next move. Society's training to always plan for the future has tricked you out of realizing the importance of the gift you have right now. The present: take a breath and enjoy it, for you may not have the chance tomorrow.

Angel Wings

Broken glass and angel wings lost in sands of time. Splinters of moon fall from the sky, landing on the backs of wolves. Pale-skinned and cold, the soulless devour the light left in the eyes of the innocent. A coven of witches watches from eight points of the world, while destruction befalls the hearts of men. Stand clear of the cemetery, for hallowed be thy ground no longer. War will reach all in the end, during the battle of mortal souls, raging since the fall of the thirteen angels beseeching the throne of God. Followers of the highest change holy words, turning church to profit by their false preachings. Many fall to greed, making holy war on other religions. All should buy a spot in heaven, say devils hidden behind white collars

D.

It seems darkness has found me again. And it was I who flipped the switch. Isn't that the way it goes? It seems that amidst this crowded room, I am unknown. Most of the time I don't even know myself. I am learning with the rest of them through my mistakes. As I travel through my little world, past mistakes shine through my window: houses I have built and roofs I have scaled. Yes, I am a broken construction worker, my blood and sweat covered by the next trade. There is no trace of my existence, for nobody can see the bones that I have constructed. Even the bricks I laid will diminish in time, for things are not built to last anymore. And now I sit alone in a last effort, for the purpose of telling stories that I hope are liked. You never know where life is going to take you, and some roads unintentionally end before they are truly traveled. Stay strong in knowing that there is a purpose for us all; you just might have to read between the lines to find it.

D.

Dawn

Death sits waiting, patiently following every step we take. We constantly fear his presence, feeling his breath on our necks, always close enough to snatch us from our bodies at any moment. Even as you carefully live out your life, trying to avoid his icy-cold grasp, eventually he will close his grip around your fragile throat, stealing the last breath from your aging body. Even if you take every precaution, staying safely out of danger, with time on his side, none escape the certainty of meeting death face to face. So accept the fact that soon this peril will befall you, and enjoy every sunrise with no intention of seeing the next dawn.

Greed

Greed is my name; hand in hand with envy and jealousy I reside. Everyone walks through my shadow. There is none I have not infected with my disease. With fits of rage, I have helped mold the world in which we live. I have been around since the first human walked the earth, and will linger 'til they walketh no longer. Through the folly of man, mindless murder over disagreements make all see my way. Countries fall under my fists, making millions suffer at the drop of my hand. Kings kneel before me; I feed off their dire lust for more and turn them to slaves. I send them to early graves at the hands of my more worthy puppets, on and on through the ages.

History Written in Blood

Written in blood, history tells us of our will to own the world: countries changing hands within decades, rulers rising and falling like the tides. Still we try to tame the untamable, only leaving our world drenched with the blood of the innocent. We fight a losing battle against an unseen enemy, pushing our people blindly into extinction. Will we ever stop the mindless slaughter of our peers, or will history simply repeat itself, as it has done ever since the first page was written? Sadly, the human race has the need to control and conquer, and that will never change.

The Line

The line we walk grows thinner every day. You may not notice the difference, for it happens ever so gracefully, stretching closer to the ground with each step. You never know if it will continue to gradually bring you to the ground, or snap with the next move, throwing you to your grave.

Roots

The soul winds through you with gnarled roots of confusion. You spend your whole life attempting to untangle the knots, trying to make sense of this life bestowed upon you, unknowing where the next root leads. You are driven by hope and navigate by karma. It matters not what you have or the number of achievements you have gained, as long as, on your last day, you can look back and say that in life you gave all you had. So live a good life and stop fiddling with the mess and distractions. The knots will unweave themselves when the time is there. Whether you know it or not, life will happen as it is supposed to for you

Small Insights

The passing of souls is intimate. You cannot hide from your pending, lonely tomb, the ultimate seclusion. The acceptance of mortality is a strengthener of spirit. Faith is not lost, just conveniently misplaced.

A new dawn is a chance to brush away the darkness. Open your mind to a new day and enjoy the crisp air of new beginnings.

Unlike the fields of crumbled, marbled stones, which are grouped together yet all alone, side by side they rot away, but I'm your diamond that never fades.

There is no certainty in the lives we live, except the fact that they will eventually come to an end.

Starry Winter

The cool, crisp air of a starry winter's night: breathe deep as it rejuvenates the soul. Do you feel small when you look to the stars, disconnected from the world and all alone? Or do you realize that you are part of the universe, a cell in the body of a greater picture? Every star, no matter how insignificant, shines in its own way within the vast night sky. Like you: even if you don't see your own sparkle, it's there for the rest of the world to see.

The Beaten Shore

Darkness floods through the world, crippling happiness with every wave. Sanity, like a shallow shore, is beaten repeatedly by the relentless tide. Simultaneously, the moon sheds light and feeds the pull of cold waters that numb our senses. The sunset is gone, the melding of day and night has now passed. And with the sun finally surrendering to the horizon, we are left ravished by darkness.

The Curse

What do you see when you look upon the stars? To me, every star that shines over your head is a reminder of the lights that I've made disappear from mortal eyes. I have been cursed upon an act of love by the ancient, vengeful God who looked upon me as a murderer for doing what I was instructed to do. Now I am in constant solitude, living forever to watch the whole world die around me, never to taste sweet death for myself except upon my lips. Every life I've taken, I wished could be mine. I stand over them and admire their peaceful faces as they pass from this world. It sometimes produces the familiar lump in the throat, but I no longer have tears to shed. You don't know how lucky you are to die, to have your pain come to a peaceful end while I'm forced to feed upon your fragile neck. I watch enviously as you drift slowly into death, dropping limp in my grasp.

The devils in the details

The devil is in the details.

Pay close attention to the surroundings in which you live, for the most subtle change can alter the very well-being of your life. The silence before the storm, so to speak, is true in nature and also in human nature. The slightest change in a smile can have a menacing intent to the unaware. The eyes tell all to ones who can read them.

Be alert to members of the human race. They are the hardest to read. Malevolence is their nature, always going for all. Never satisfied, they always hunger for the ultimate reward, ready to smite any who get in their way. From the rich tycoon reaching for the top to the addict reaching for the ultimate high, nothing will alter their chase. The higher they get, the more cunning they become.

In a way, we all are vampires, draining strengths by learning weaknesses. We prey on those who are ignorant of the signs of deceit. Just as animals are tethered as bait on the spot where the hunter waits, the weak are baited by the ones thirsting for power. Their consciences have been tricked by their evils, as they conveniently make all right in their own minds. Hence the phrase, "It's nothing personal, just business." In all reality, it most certainly is personal to both them and you.

As I said before, the devil's in the details, whether it's moods, body language, or the trickery of the businessman's fine print. All is there if you train yourself to be aware. Of all the creatures on the planet, it's the humans who are the deadliest of them all.

The Mirror

Every day, a stranger is looking back at you. You don't recognize this person, never guessing this shell standing before you houses the same feelings you hold deep within yourself. You are unable to run from this stranger; he is always there, peering through you.

Try to change your weight, looks, or hair; still, there he is, trying to gain your acceptance, mocking your changes, looking more and more distant, ageing and changing right by your side.

Can he ever be embraced? Is it possible to accept this ever-present stranger you spend your whole life fighting? You flip through the pages of existence, hoping he just goes away—only to cross his path wherever a reflection is possible.

Stop fighting and realize that the stranger is you. No matter what you do, forever locked inside is the unchangeable you. So next time you pass yourself by, stop for a moment and say hi to that stranger looking back at you. Stop the battle you just can't win, and finally embrace that stranger within. Together, you will find happiness, for your soul knows no other way.

The shore

The moon sinks into a distant horizon, looking as if it had fallen into the sea. Take not the tide, for it clears the rough beach ahead. It leaves gifts from the dark ocean floor, though never to breathe again; erases thy footprints along the sand, an hourglass that never needs turning; wipes the beach clean with every rise of the new day. Wake anew this day with hope of clear waters. Still and calm, they whisper to those who listen of ancient tales and warnings. Make not the mistakes of those whose steps were taken before you as you walk along the new, blank shore.

The Tear

The moonlight falls upon a single tear, a perfect drop of sadness falling from the eye of regret. Softly mourn past differences and decisions gone by. Look more into what was learned than remaining stuck with the confusions of the question why. Feast upon knowledge; fear not for today. Its dawn comes upon you and will not go away. When given your present of each brand-new day, the past is the price not intended to pay. Featured through now if you learned from you then, the future withholds a personal win. Your spirit grows strong; its roots runneth deep when the moonlight shines through the regret that you weep.

The Waste

He stands beside himself, his ink-stained body slowly falling apart. Can you hear God? Can you feel the light when the bulb has burned out? When you don't send ripples through the soul, it becomes stagnant, creating a breeding ground for depression. Seeds of failure crawl through his chemically lined veins. Now he is only a provider of heartache and hurt. He feels love and devotion bursting in his chest, yet somehow it leaves his body in mixed messages of change and confusion, which in turn slowly make his beloved walk backward into the shadows. He chases his beloved and holds on with all that he is worth, but his hands are failing. Where is God now? Can she see him anymore, or has the ink diluted the purity of his soul? Perhaps it's just his fate to feel that he amounts to nothing in the scheme of life: always a lesson to everyone but never to feel the joys of one day being the answer.

The Wounded Soul

It is not the time to overlook the complexity of the wounded soul. The soul flickers like a lantern about to extinguish. Delivering and receiving pain is a poison, slowly diminishing the illumination of thyself as the flame weakens. It's easy to see exactly what feeds the light and what shadows the intensity. Sometimes acknowledging the self-mutilation brought on by the beholder will shock the soul, rendering the body numb and emotionless. Accept the anger of being at fault and the scar tissue it holds. To see and know the worth within will turn the scars to magnificent patterns of strength and mosaic love, patterns that can be read even by the blind and achieve growth at a rate noticeable to the angels. It's time to feed the soul … it's time to hang on.

Thirst of the Tyrant

With a wave of his hand, thousands of men have fallen. Safely at the rear of his armies, he watches and plans his next wave of death. Even against their will and better judgment, his loyal puppets erase everything in their path. Throughout the pages of time, some choose to rise against these tyrants or give their lives in failed efforts to stop the disease from spreading. Many heroes and brave men go unrecognized, for against the kings of the world, few have been left to tell of their sacrifices. From kings to presidents, the puppets still push through history, stealing sons from the grip of weeping mothers. Armed only through prayer, the heroes survive the thirst of their king.

Time

The days press on whether we are ready or not; that's one of the many things in our lives that we can't change. It is impossible to take an hourglass and turn it on its side, stopping time. Even when an individual heart stops beating, time still presses for the remainder of the world. The time of your extinction starts in the second of conception. So, in a sense, we are all riding the countdown to death, never knowing exactly when our moment will arrive.

At the end of our moments, we realize that, no matter the marks we leave upon the world, they will slowly erode with time. It is the healer of all wounds. All the pains and cuts fester and slowly scar over with every passing second of our brief existence. So use your limited time in this world carefully, because that's exactly what it is, limited. Do what counts. Be a teacher to those you encounter. Don't try to carve your mark on the world, for in the long run, marks fade. Instead, concentrate on leaving an impression on the people that you love. They in turn will take your teachings and examples, passing those down to the ones that they love. When time goes on and the world changes hands, even though you are forgotten, the imprints you made will help mold a better tomorrow for the generations yet to come.

Transformation

Watch as we shed our ideas like a snake shedding its skin, only for new outlooks on the plane in which we temporarily dwell. Go ahead: stand in the mortuary waiting your turn to evolve. Do you really think you get wings in the end? Are you too blind to see them now, perched upon your crooked back? Stand straight and spread your arms, deeply inhaling the cold winter air. Look around: nature sleeps, and her trees are imitating death.

The stars have been dead for years. Do you still live in the memory of their light, or can you create your own? You will never find God if you can't understand that she is spread through the world in every living thing. Wake up, see the freak show of life in a different light. Find the beauty in chaos and manipulate the dreary visions forced upon you by the masses. Then you will truly see. Come on in, we've been waiting for you.

Whispers in the mist

Stand for a moment. Just stand silently to absorb the moment. This is a moment that you will want to remember. Wherever it is that you are, you will benefit from taking in the breath of this moment. Listen to the million things happening simultaneously that were too small to notice before: the light breeze tickling the tall weeds surrounding an old tomb; the trees moaning as the ground settles. Watch as the setting sun shines through the remains of stained glass in a mausoleum door. The shadows of the past are bleeding upon your feet as the rays of yesterday's sun make their final reach from a darkening horizon. They are calling out for you with whispers in the mist.

Here are the first few chapters of my novel *Cain*.

It surprises me that no one really touches on Cain and Abel. There's too much romance and kung fu fighting today. In this novel, I want the reader to see that becoming a vampire is not something that you want to happen in your life. Think about this: you are punished by being forced to roam the earth forever. All your feelings are intact, and everyone you know or will ever know will die around you. You are unable to make more of your kind. To be truly alone was the biblical punishment. With every life you take, which you must do, you see and feel the very first, the life of your brother. It is an eternal sorrow of which you are forever reminded. Cain was never to rest, for in the original punishment he was branded by God himself that none should kill him. That's right, not holy water or wooden stakes, not even the sun. In this story, there is no way out, just as God intended.

These are the chapters of the fall of Abel—the brothers' bond and betrayal, so to speak. And just to make it clear, even though I used biblical sources, this story is fiction. It's out of my head, so don't bother looking up time lines or facts on the areas where the events take place. The only facts at all are that Cain loved Abel, and Cain murdered Abel. I have tried to find out more, but unfortunately the Bible has been picked apart and translated so many times that there's only two or three paragraphs left. They must have had to make room for the parts on how much you have to give the church to buy a seat in heaven.

Which, just in case you were wondering, you don't have to do. In fact, the only thing I got out of that book was that Jesus was a man, not a god. And he was a smart man who said church is wherever you are, hiding under every stone.

With that, I hope you enjoy my story. I will publish the rest upon finishing.

Cain: The First Drop
Chapter One

I am Cain and my story is as old as time. Biblical, as you might say. I am a vampire, although I was not always this way. I had a normal life just like yours once. I was a farmer who loved the fields, the way the breeze tickled the crops. Night and day, I would work them. They were all I had. Well, them and my brother Abel. Abel worked with the animals. He loved the animals just as much as I loved the fields. Often I would help him take care of his flock.

One day I was tilling, and Abel came to me with one of his animals. It was a small horse. He said it was a gift to help me in the fields. I should have taken it, especially knowing what I do now, but I denied the gift. "My fields are small, Brother, and I love to work the land myself."

He looked at me for a while and replied, "You need company out here, don't you? Don't you get lonely out here? All day long you stand in these fields."

"Listen to the wind, Brother. Can you hear it whisper as it runs through the wheat?"

He stood quietly for a moment. "All I hear is this horse breathing on my shoulder."

I smiled at him and laughed. "Exactly!" I told him, as I patted him on his shoulder.

"Okay, then, you go ahead and listen to your whispering fields, just don't start whispering back. And bring some vegetables in tonight for dinner." He started to walk away, then turned and said, "Don't bring any vegetables that whisper." He turned back and continued to walk away.

That is how it was all the time; we got along great. We ate well. Abel provided the meat, and I brought the fruits and vegetables. I had relatively small fields, but there were many, and I grew anything I could. Once I had thirty small fields, which turned out to be a little much, both for me and the cellar. I hated to see things spoil, especially my back. So I learned to keep it at about fifteen fields, including my fruits and berries. I also learned to dry things and put them in leather bags that my brother made me. He was always helping me out.

Together, we built two barns and a nursery for all of Abel's animals. His flock, like my fields, continued to grow. We would joke around quite often, working through the whole day without really knowing where the time went. We would always stop to watch the sunset. Every dusk was a wonder. The sky would explode in reds and golds. It wasn't out of the ordinary for us to lie on the ground and watch the whole thing without saying a word.

Other times we would talk, about normal things, I guess: our dreams and plans for the future. Abel would talk most of the time; he had a lot more to say. Often he talked about his animals. He had close bonds with all of them. It seemed like they were his children. He had names for them all; it was hard to keep up, really. Not to mention the way he talked about all the things each animal did all day, like they were human.

"You spend too much time with those animals. Listen to yourself carry on," I often said.

"You're just jealous, your corn just stands around," he said, imitating my plants with a stupid expression painted on his face.

Like I said, life wasn't boring. There was hardly a dull moment. I would have to tell him frequently to get his children out of my fields–mainly his chickens and ducks. I would yell and scream. The chickens didn't like it, but the ducks! Every time I turned my back, they would charge me, sneak attack. Sometimes I would catch myself playing with them, kind of red light, green light, because every time I turned and faced them, they would stop like they weren't up to anything. During times of boredom, it was fun, but I never let Abel know: he would never have let me live it down.

Truth be told, I had animals of my own. I quite enjoyed the birds' company, and when I stood still enough, deer would just about come up to me. In fact, I knew all the wild animals and even watched them bring up their children. I watched them grow up and bring up their own families. My brother didn't know that, either; like I said, he would never have let me live it down.

We spent a lot of time together since we didn't have to leave our fields much. There was not a lot of need to go to town except for building material or clothes; everything else we provided ourselves. My crops fed his animals, and in return I had all the fertilizer I needed. When we needed money, we would sell our extras. People said I had the best crops around. Even Abel's animals were well taken care of, not like a lot of the other animals in the market. We loved what we did, and there was a harmony to it, poetic really. Not like a lot of others who had more than they could take good care of, undernourished and sickly animals and crops. That's why, when we wanted to sell, there were instantaneous results.

I remember that we would wait sometimes until we heard how everyone was fed up with the quality of the items in the market. Then we would announce that we had extra, and people would bombard our farm. We really got a kick out of it sometimes.

Sure, we had regulars that we would take care of. There were the elders of the town, some widowed, others just up in years. Abel would often watch them; that was sometimes top conversation during our sunset watch. He really wanted to find a mate to grow old with, someone other than me. It's not like he didn't try or anything, but he was too involved with his animals. He said that it would happen when it was time. Abel was like that; he had a strong belief in things like karma and fate, which were other common conversation pieces of his.

Abel was a strong man in very good shape. He was a little shorter than me but just as strong. All farmers are, really; it's hard work. Weather, animals, or crops, it takes its toll on you. Sure, you learn how to make your jobs easier on yourself, but even then it is physically demanding.

Every time I went to hoe my fields, it seemed there were rocks. I collected them for our building purposes. In fact, I lined our cellar with them, and most of our house was covered in stone. It made a much stronger home than just having wood. Also, it made me very strong. That was good; I liked the fact that when Abel got squirrely, I could easily take him down.

He was okay with the fact that I was a little stronger than him, although he still tried wrestling around, using the element of surprise. Little did he know that his ducks had helped me learn to judge how close something was behind me. Plus, my hearing was great; I knew every sound in my surroundings, and Abel was not a very quiet person. I would almost hear him think of trying to sneak up on me. I would just keep on working, pretending that I had no idea of his even being there.

Once he was pursuing me after a long rain. As usual, I heard him the moment he entered the field. Earlier, I had noticed a pretty big mud puddle, so I wandered over, looking at the ears of corn, placing myself right in front of the puddle. Abel stood there, waiting for the perfect moment. I turned slightly. He was sure that he was undiscovered when really I was just placing him in my peripheral vision. I noticed him smile; he really thought that he had me. I looked down to see an ear of corn that had been half-eaten by a deer. I bent to pick it from the stalk, keeping Abel in my sight. Thinking that he was finally going to surprise me, he bounced, then lunged at me headfirst. As soon as I realized there was no stopping his action, I simply stepped to the side.

Abel, covered in mud, was looking at me, shocked and silent. He said, "You knew I was there, didn't you? You set me up!" Frustration was building in his eyes.

"Nooo," I said, fighting a smile. "How could I have known? You snuck up on me."

"Right," he said with high amounts of sarcasm, wiping mud from his soaked clothes. Then he looked at me with a crooked smile running across his face.

"Don't you do it," I said. Then, out of nowhere, he tackled me. It was the only time I didn't see it coming, probably because I was laughing myself to tears. When Abel pulled us both into the mud, we were both soaked, but it was worth the look on his face. Little did we know life was about to change.

Chapter Two

It was storming that night, the lightning constantly lighting up the sky with short flickers. I got out of bed to make sure the shutters were latched tightly. As I looked out the kitchen window, I noticed a lantern was lit in Abel's barn. Throwing on an overcoat, I walked to the barn to see what he was doing.

Apparently the storm had scared one of his sheep, putting her into an early labor. Abel was comforting her, trying to keep her from giving birth. Even I knew there was a chance the lamb wouldn't survive if it was born this early, and I don't know too much about that stuff. I went to Abel's side, trying to keep him calm; he was looking just as bad as the poor sheep. For a long time, we were in that barn. I kept talking to him, trying to ease his mind, but I was unsuccessful. He was too worried about his friend. I could see the concern in his eyes, and I knew my brother very well, so at that point I knew the best thing for him was my support. I stood silently next to him with my hand upon his shoulder.

It was like that for some time. I stood watching the rain illuminated by lightning. Abel tried his best to comfort his sheep, stroking her head as she lay there upon the straw. The poor thing would shake with every roar of thunder, which came all too often that night. Her eyes were fixed upon the barn door. Seeing this, I walked over and shut it to ease her mind. It didn't have the effect I was hoping for. The door still rattled violently from the heavy winds, which really disturbed the sheep. There really wasn't anything either of us could do; she was terrified, eyes locked upon the door as if she could see something that we couldn't. Her nostrils flared from her erratic breathing.

"Cain, come quick," Abel called out. My eyes were still fixed upon the door, trying to see what spooked her. "She's going into labor. Hold her down."

I snapped out of my trance and went to assist my brother. Bending down, I tried holding the sheep's front legs to keep her from kicking. With every crack of thunder, her hooves sank beneath the straw, trenching the soil underneath. I had to apply all my strength just to hold the animal down. Feelings of remorse flooded through me. My head was next to hers as my body held her top half down.

Then a few things happened almost simultaneously. The sheep let out a sigh. This was no ordinary sigh. I was talking to her in an attempt to sooth her, and we were almost eye to eye. During that moment when she sighed, she gave birth, and I swear I could see the light in her giant eyes diminish. It was one of the saddest things I had encountered.

Abel was unaware of what had just occurred. He called out, "It's a girl, it's a girl, good job." He went to congratulate her by patting her shoulder, and that's when he realized what had happened.

I placed my hand atop his, looking sympathetically into his eyes. "She passed as she gave birth. I'm sorry, Brother."

His eyes started to well up. He grabbed a cloth tarp from the stable wall, covering his friend and patting her as he whispered, "I'm gonna miss you, girl." Then he rose. I walked over to him. In silence, we stood looking down at the tarp that covered the poor animal. Abel said, "Will you help me bury her when the ground dries?"

I put my hand upon his shoulder. "Of course I will."

With that, he grabbed the newborn lamb, held it against his wounded heart, he pulled open the door with his free hand and ran through the rain, taking the lamb into the house.

I stood in the barn for some time I didn't know how to cope with the sadness. I felt for that poor creature. The intensity of seeing a soul escape a living creature was hard to take. I still wondered what she had been staring at. Was it the storm or something else? All I could do was stand there, lost in thought.

The storm started to lose its intensity. It was now just a light sprinkle. I opened the door to the barn and sat on a bale of straw next to the sheep. I was mesmerized by the spot of the sheep's last gaze. "It must have just been the storm," I thought. With that, I stepped out of the barn door, closing it behind me, looking at the sheep as the door closed.

I didn't want to be in the barn anymore. I also wasn't ready to go in the house yet, so I decided to stand in the now drizzling rain. The moon was making an appearance between passing clouds. I again was lost in thought while standing next to the house. I didn't hear any movement inside, and decided to go in and get some sleep.

The next morning was quiet. Abel hardly spoke and neither did I. He had the new lamb in a wooden box upon the kitchen floor.

I watched her as he got some eggs for breakfast. We ate in silence, then I went to tend my fields.

The storm the previous night had been strong. It ravaged my fields: stalks were broken and my crop was everywhere. It was going to take a while to clean up. The ground was too wet to work.

I could see Abel moping around. His chores had to be done regardless, so I figured that my mess could wait. I told Abel to tend to his new lamb. I could tell he was concerned about her. As I tended his flock, I realized why he felt so strongly about his animals. They were kind of like people in a way. They were happy for my companionship, their tails wagging, nudging me for attention. After a couple days, I started to have a bond with them. I even had an excuse to play with the ducks.

The ground finally dried out, and Abel was ready to bury his friend. He had already constructed a box for her. Any other time, I would have thought it a little much, but after being one on one with his animals the past few days, I understood his kindness for them a little more. After all, that sheep had been with him for a long time.

We carried the pine box to the hill that overlooked my fields, the place where we watched the sunset every night. It was a short burial. I dug most of the grave. That's what I was good at, so it didn't take me long. I did notice, however, that I put a lot of care into this particular hole. We lowered the box and Abel said a few words, then I comforted him and said that I would finish the burial. He took one last, long look upon the grave and said, "Thanks," as he walked into the house. I think it would have been too much for him.

After covering the box with soil, I sat atop the hill next to her fresh grave. Dusk started to fall, and Abel strolled slowly out to the hill, sitting next to me.

"Thanks, Brother. I couldn't have done this without you."

"Don't mention it. That's what family does," I told him. Then, we watched the sunset in silence. The sunset was spectacular that evening. Clouds moved fast, gathering the intense red-gold colors and dropping them, regaining the original darkness they once held.

In the following days, things started to regain a sense of normality. I was tending to my fields again, and Abel was back with his animals. His new lamb was constantly at his side. The lamb reminded me of a white, puffy dog. It was pretty comical, really, the instant bond they had. I watched them sometimes while I was in the fields.

I helped Abel more than usual now that I knew his animals better. There were even times that I looked forward to helping him out. Things really got back on track when he tried sneaking up on me again. I let him take me by surprise a few times. Things were better; the wounds were scarring over.

Abel was perceptibly back to normal. He was chattering, and the new lamb joined us on our sunset watches. "What are you going to call her?" I asked while stroking her head.

"Powder," he said simply, joining me in petting her.

"Powder, huh? That's a good name for her," I replied, and we sat watching the sunset, petting Powder, until the sun disappeared into the horizon.

Chapter Three

Although things were normal at home now, there was a change about the whole atmosphere. Things were happening all around us. We just didn't realize the effect it was going to have on our lives.

Abel and Powder took the wagon into town to get the things we needed. I decided not to go that day, figuring that I could get things done. With my helping Abel lately, my fields hadn't gotten their proper attention. Some of the crop was ruined from the storm; I wasn't really sure that there was going to be enough to last 'til next season. I tried to salvage as much as I could from the ground. To my surprise, it looked like the majority of the crop was still good. It just wasn't in the same spot where it had been planted. I couldn't believe it: there was corn thrown at least thirty feet away. It took me a while to seek out all the crop in its new location.

While I was lost in my work, I couldn't help but notice the placement of the sun. It was getting late, and I wondered what was taking Abel so long. I gathered my broken stalks and other debris from the fields, making a fire in the far corner. That's when I saw Abel and Powder on their way back in from town.

I made sure my fire was under control and walked over to the house. With the speed they were traveling, I easily made it to the house by the time they did, ready to help unload the supplies. "You were gone a long time," I told him, smiling, glad to see him return home safely.

He looked at me with kind of a half-crooked smile. "Yeah, we made it," he said. There was something different in his eyes that day, something that I had never seen before. I asked him what was wrong, but he had no reply. He simply avoided my query and started to unload the supplies. So instead of pushing the issue, I decided to let it go and just help unload. He had brought the usual things; there wasn't anything odd—other than Abel, that is. It looked like he had lost part of his soul. He was pale, and his eyes were sunken in and dull. I was concerned. I had never seen him that way.

Days passed and it seemed that he never regained his color. Also, he missed our sunset watch, although Powder joined me. That was nice, because I had grown quite fond of her. I didn't have the bond Abel had, of course. He loved that animal. In fact, it was odd for her to be on the hill without him. Powder and I sat for some time until it was obvious that Abel wasn't joining us.

Patting Powder on the head, I went into the house to see what had happened to him. As I walked in, there he was, sitting in the middle of the floor, rocking slightly back and forth with his head in his hands.

"Abel, what's wrong?"

"God," he said.

"God?" I replied. "What are you talking about?"

"He's talking to me, he is in my head," he said while grasping his hair and pulling. Tears started to roll down his pale face.

"What? You're just ill or something. Here, let me get you off the floor." I reached down to help him up.

"No, leave me, I'm not ill. You don't understand, he's in my head."

"What is he saying?" I asked.

He looked up at me, his eyes receding into their sockets. His lips were cracked and dry, while the rest of his face bore a corpse-like appearance. He forced a frown and whispered through his teeth, "Sacrifice."

I stood there, bewilderment stretching across my face. Seeing him like this broke my heart in two. It was tearing him up from the inside out; I could literally see his soul dissipate. The tears were freely flowing now, and his rocking intensified. I tried again to assist him. Caringly, I bent down and put my hand around his arm. He pulled away, ripping his arm from my grasp. He looked at me with malice in his eyes, not saying a word.

I stood up in shock. All that I could do was step away and watch him as he rocked on the floor. The light of the torch was eerily flickering upon his crooked body as he whispered over and over, "Sacrifice. God wants sacrifice." I watched intently as I slowly backed out the door.

I returned to the hill. The sun was nearly all the way down and the starry night sky was taking its place. There was a shadow now to my far right. Powder was still there, perched in the same spot, slightly trembling from the cold.

"Come now, little lamb. We will take shelter in the barn tonight." We walked slowly to the barn. As we approached the door, I turned and gave a last look at the house. Abel's shadow was cast on the wall of main room. I could see him through the window-slits, still rocking. I said a prayer for him, then turned away to open the barn door. The big door creaked as I pushed it open. The breeze it created stirred the dust on the barn floor.

As I grabbed a lantern from a hook upon the wall and set a match to it, the first thing that caught my attention was the spot where Powder was born. I could still feel the last breath of her mother upon my cheek. I sat on that spot with my little friend, stroking her young wool. Then I cast my attention on the door, the last spot that held her mother's eye. I swore I could see a shadow. I couldn't place it; never had I seen such a shape. It didn't seem to be mortal. As I tried to make it out, it was gone.

Quickly, I turned. Fear was pulsing through my body. There was nothing there. I shook my head, figuring that if I wasn't careful, I, too, would drift into insanity.

That again made me think of my brother alone in the house, obviously losing his mind.

Powder and I must have drifted off to sleep. The brisk coldness of the late-night air woke me. Powder was still slumbering at my side. Nudging the lamb away, I quietly snuck out, careful not to wake the young animal. I was worried about my brother, and I had to check on him.

The sky was clear that night, making it cold, but the stars were breathtaking. I couldn't help but notice them dance overhead. As

I approached the house, it seemed wise for me to look into the window-slits rather than just walking in. The torch had burned out, making it almost impossible to peer inside. After a deep breath, I made my way to the front of the house, ever so carefully pushing the door ajar.

To my surprise, Abel was no longer in the main room. Silence filled the empty space. Cautiously I stood, hardly breathing while listening for sound, any sound at that moment. The very air was still, heavy, and dark. Even the regular sounds of night seemed to hold their breath.

Tension slowly worked its way up my spine. Why did I hold that fear inside? There were messages of warning that I did not comprehend. Even while I let myself think that there was no need to fear my brother, something deep within my gut beckoned me to stay alert. My senses were heightened; the quiet was scary all in itself. Any noise at that moment would have given me a heart attack for sure.

I searched the remainder of the house. Abel was nowhere. I went back outside, the eerie feeling still lingering. Standing in front of the door, I slowly glanced around the property, looking for any movement. Darkness was the only thing that could be seen. That was odd because, upon entering the house, I remembered that the stars had been gleaming overhead, creating a glow on the earth, making sight at least somewhat possible. I again looked to the heavens. There was nothing. The sky was empty. "How could this happen?" I thought to myself. It had not taken that long to search the house for my brother. Yet within that time, it looked as if someone had stolen every star from the night sky.

It was almost like a dream, looking back at it all now. Nothing seemed real, every detail of that night somehow distorted. It didn't take long for the silence to break. Powder brayed in the background. It was so quiet that night that her soft voice carried like a scream. While hurrying for the animal, I nearly tripped from the lack of light. Again the baby animal made an alarming sound, and as I neared the barn, it was clear that she was no longer there. The door was wide open, and I knew it had been shut before.

"Abel," I thought. But where was he?

Just then a noise rang through the night. It sounded like it came from the hill. From the barn, the distance to the hill was close to one hundred feet. Regardless of the dark, I had to hurry. It didn't matter if I fell ten times. There was a feeling of urgency rushing over my body in a sudden wave.

I started to sprint toward the hill. The darkness was interrupted by sudden flashes of heat lightning. Within the flashes, I could see Abel standing over Powder.

"*Abel, no!*" I yelled as I closed in on the last thirty feet of my sprint. Another flash; I was almost right on top of them now. I was horrified when I finally approached them. The sudden flash illuminated a makeshift altar. Abel must have started working on it as soon as I drifted off to sleep in the barn. When we had unloaded the wagon earlier, I was so concerned about the way Abel was acting that I didn't notice the extra building supplies.

He had the lamb on her side, her feet bound together and her body tied to the altar, making it impossible for her to escape. Another quick flash lit up the sky, and a heaviness fell upon us. I could see a small knife shimmering in the flash. Acting as promptly as I could, I grabbed Abel's arm. "Stop, Abel, what are you doing?"

He turned and looked at me. I could hardly recognize him. There were chunks of hair missing in random spots across his skull. His skin was pale and clammy, his eyes almost completely sunken in their sockets. Yanking his arm from my grasp, he said, "This is God's will. I must sacrifice."

The strength he possessed frightened me; for our whole lives, I had always been able to overpower him. Now, when I needed that strength most, there was a fear in me that I would not prevail in this battle. Another flash, and the knife gleamed like a star as he raised it over his head.

I looked at Powder, her eyes wide with fear. *"No, I won't let you!"* I screamed. I grabbed at his arm again. Rain suddenly started to fall on us in a sheet, making it hard for me to hang on to my brother's arm.

Angry with me now, he shook, trying to free his arm from my grasp. He was screaming, "Don't make me kill you instead!"

I couldn't even respond; he had never yelled at me before. His strength was alarming. I was scared to death. It was certain that if he freed his arm, Powder was dead. I held on to Abel with all the strength that I could muster.

It was not enough. He freed his arm and went for the lamb. Again I grabbed for him, the heavy rain making every grasp difficult. He turned back, making eye contact. Pure malice was in his eyes. *"You dare defy God's will?"*

Tears flooded my eyes, mixing with the rain as I pleaded. "Please stop, Brother. God would never ask someone to kill. Think about it. Put the knife down, please, Brother. Don't do this."

"It has to be done. I will not tell you again."

"Then you have to kill me first. I will not stand by and let you kill this innocent creature!"

With a blank expression on his face, like every emotion had been erased from his being, he replied, "So be it, then," and lunged at me, knife in hand. His attack was so quick that I failed to properly block. The blade cut deep into my right shoulder.

I yelled out in pain and he was on me again. This time I

managed to grab his arm. The rain made my grip slide to his wrist. He punched me in the jaw. His strength was frightening; a couple more blows like that and he would surely knock me out. I tried to shake it off, still struggling with his knife hand. His fist flew at me again, and lucky for me, this one missed.

I grabbed his other hand. We struggled face to face, his face clenched in rage, staring into my eyes as he slowly overpowered me. There was nothing else that I could do. He was going to kill me. He had obviously gone mad.

I unclenched my muscles enough for him to fall into me. As his body collided with mine, I bit into his neck. I bit so violently that it tore through his main artery, my teeth still latched, tangled in the muscle and tendon. I could not let go. His heart was pumping with such force that his blood was racing down my throat. The intense pain made him drop the knife. He went limp, falling to his knees and leaving a chunk of his neck still in my mouth.

"O God, Abel, I'm sorry, you wouldn't stop!" Immediately, I tried to stop the bleeding. I did not mean to inflict such a wound. I loved my brother. All I wanted to do was get the knife away and restrain him.

The rain was making the bleeding more intense. His strength was gone. I fell to the ground; what had I done? His color was fading fast, the light in his eyes started to darken. I had him cradled in my lap, trying to close the gaping wound with my hand.

It was too late. My brother died in my arms by my own hand.

His blood was mixing with the rain, puddling all around me, staining my clothes. I wish that I had just let him kill me. The pain of causing his demise was worse than dying myself. For what is life after the moment of knowing you have killed someone you love?

"I'm sorry, Brother," I said as I lay him down upon the wet ground. I stood looking toward the altar, seeing red liquid covering the top and washing down the sides. Before turning to attack me, Abel had quickly plunged his knife into Powder, staining her powder-white wool to a dark crimson. Two souls were lost that night, and it was all my fault. The only thing I could do was sit there in the mud and blood, falling apart. Abel was all I had. To this day, that is my biggest regret. His death truly hollowed my heart.

Chapter Four

I sat in the mud mourning the death of my brother. A numbness overcame my body. I couldn't even feel the rain anymore. Abel's body lay lifeless next to me; just to the right of him lay his knife. I stared at it for a long time, the cold steel blinking with every lightning flash. I leaned over, picking it up from the mud.

Just as I was about to thrust it into my chest, a thin bolt of lightning struck the blade, knocking it from my hand. It sent a painful shock that nearly threw me from the spot where I was sitting.

Out of nowhere, the rain ceased to fall. The sting was still pulsating through my body. The pain was growing with every passing second.

"*Cain*." The voice thundered from all around me. Panic instantly engulfed all my senses. I scurried to the makeshift altar, hoping to hide. My breathing rapidly increased. My back was pressed against the wooden altar so hard that it tipped over. It tumbled down the wet hill with Powder's body still attached.

"*Cain. Stand and be recognized*." Again the thundering voice came from all directions. I was too frightened to stand. The pain of the lightning intensified because of my delay, sending violent shocks through my whole body.

Another thin bolt came from the sky, striking the ground next to me. I realized that this was intended to make me stand. "So be it," I thought. "What could happen?" I wanted to die anyhow; at least this way I wouldn't have to do it myself. Suicide is an unforgivable sin; however, so is murder. Abel's death had been a tragic accident, though, and there was no way God would punish me for an accident.

A ray of light shone down on me. Somehow it was different from the lightning. The light was burning my flesh. The pain was unbearable. I tried to avoid the light, but it followed me, growing hotter every time I tried to evade it. My body was stiff. I was completely unable to move. The burning light held me slightly suspended off the ground.

A glow caught my attention from the other side of the hill. It started off pale, then grew in intensity, finally going out completely. I followed the glow, but it was hard for me to concentrate through the pain I was encountering.

"Would you like it to stop?" A soft, calming voice surrounded me, not coming from any particular direction. It seemed to be coming from inside my head, telepathically.

"Who said that?" I answered.

"Do not question me, mortal," said the voice, growing more irritated. The pain completely overtook me. Regaining the original comforting tone, it said again, "Would you like it to stop?"

The pain now was excruciating. I could hardly form a word. "Yes," I muttered.

In an instant, the pain ceased, as did the light. Still I remained suspended, unable to move. "Thank you," I said, relieved. It was amazing that all my pain stopped, even the cut upon my right shoulder.

A shape finally passed over the hill, coming into view. I could not believe my eyes. It was unlike anything I had ever witnessed. The figure that approached me was flawless. He wore strange clothing, metallic in the sense that it resembled armor. Over the armor, he wore a golden-colored material perfectly draped over his tall, slender frame. He almost looked fragile, yet he carried himself like a force of reckoning.

The oddest but most beautiful feature he bore was great wings folded on his back. Like the material, his wings had a golden hue about them. It looked as if he was a child of the sun; he even had a faint glow that covered his whole body.

"I am an archangel. My name is Ariel, and it is my duty to punish or reward the actions of mankind." Ariel's words softly swarmed in my head, yet his lips did not move.

Ariel noticed the look upon my face. I was going to speak, but I did not want to question him anymore. Even with the beauty of this angel, the pain he could instantly turn on and off was to be feared.

"I do not have to move my mouth as mortals do, for I am not mortal." He almost seemed pleased at my uneasiness.

His eyes were different, I noticed as he looked into mine. They were also golden: no whites or pupils, just a solid shade of gold.

You would think that would scare me at first glance, but oddly enough, it was beautiful just like the rest of him, a calming sight to behold.

He slowly stepped away, studying the scene before him and glancing at me from time to time with a disappointed and confused look upon his perfect face.

As he walked, I couldn't help but speak. "Haven't I seen you before?" I said cautiously, fearing that he would induce the pain again.

He stopped instantly. Swiftly, he turned his attention back to me. His eyes flashed as he tilted his head. "The living do not see us." His voice had a sarcasm to it as it rang in my head.

"The shadow in the barn—its shape resembled yours."

His glance quickly turned to a menacing glare. Ariel's eyes turned to a dark color that I can't even explain. But the feeling that came with the change warned me not to risk trying to speak again.

He walked over to me, mere inches from my face. "My purpose is to judge and to punish. You should not taunt me."

"Punish? I was trying to save Powder and disarm my brother.

This was an accident." I did not understand why this was happening to me.

Ariel studied my face. Swiftly he turned, grabbing Abel's body and bringing him over to me. "This is your accident?" he said, his eyes wide as he stared directly into mine.

I could not believe what I saw. The man he brought to me was the real Abel, not the pale, insane Abel I had left lying in the mud. There in front of me was the brother that I had known and loved my whole life. I wanted to cry, but oddly, it was impossible.

I shifted my glance upon Ariel. "You don't understand. He went mad. His appearance was even different. This is not the man he was."

Ariel was annoyed with this. He rested Abel's body back upon the muddy ground and walked behind me. He then reappeared carrying yet another body. "It was you who was mad. You murdered your brother in cold blood."

Then he lifted the body to my view. It was me. My body was pale and thin, my eyes sunken and dark, the blade lodged in my chest.

The very second that I looked into my lifeless, sunken eyes, my mind snapped. I remembered everything. The whole thing played very fast, almost too fast to even comprehend. The flood of insight started the night of Powder's birth. The images that rushed through me were terrifying. I could not believe it. Incomplete bursts of disturbing images showing me killing Powder's mother, snapping her neck as I helped Abel in the barn. Then I was burning my fields, locking Abel and Powder out of the house, destroying everything in my path.

The vision shifted to me rocking on the floor, fast and violent, constructing the altar, sneaking into the barn, grabbing Powder while Abel slept next to her, tying her to the altar, then going back for my brother. I stabbed him in his sleep, keeping him alive but paralyzed so he could not resist.

The next burst was brutal. I witnessed myself setting my brother in front of the altar as I cut his lamb's throat. Finally, walking to my helpless brother, I violently ripped through his neck with my teeth, then walked over the hill and plunged my knife into my chest.

I screamed. It was all my fault. And now I could not deny it.

Without any warning, the angel cupped his hand and thrust it toward me. What followed was excruciating. I fell to my knees. Nothing but pain surrounded me. All my senses were screaming for release, though I feared there was none to be had. It only lasted moments, but it felt eternal.

I was kneeling in the mud, yet the cold did not penetrate my skin. I tried to shake it off. Was I dead, or were my senses failing due to the intensity of the torture that I endured?

The archangel spoke, his words soft again in my mind. "Your nerve endings are gone. Never again will you feel the rain upon your face or the touch of another soul."

I was still looking down at my knees in the mud. I held my hands in front of me, pressing my palms down to the dirt. I could see my hands disappear into the puddle before me, and yet I could not feel the sensations that I was accustomed to. "I am dead," I thought to myself.

"You are most certainly not dead. In fact, death is a reward that you will never see."

The words lingered in my head, silently echoing in my brain. I lifted my hands from the water. The falling rain washed the mud from them as I lifted them, turning my palms to my face. That's when I noticed the brands burned into my palms.

"You are marked, marked eternally for the brutality you inflicted here upon this hill. You have brought murder into this world. Now, from your example, there will be war and suffering, man killing man, brother killing brother. And you, Cain, you will witness it all," he said softly as he walked to where I was kneeling.

He put his hand down. Whether he touched me, I do not know, but I saw his hand coming down from the corner of my eye. Quickly I flinched away, not wanting any more abuse. I scurried back to the fallen altar, crouching before him.

"You will always thirst, yet blood is all you will drink. You will always hunger, yet ash is all you will taste. You will long for death, yet eternity is all you will receive. Thus it is done." He held his hands out to his sides and brought them together in front of him. In a flash, he was gone.

I looked upon my hands, then to the sky. There I sat, and the sun came and went many times before I even moved. When I stood, the ground did not push against my feet, yet I was standing. I could not feel the sun on my skin even as I watched it glisten. I held my bare arm out into a direct ray; still no sensation befell me.

My head fell, and there he was in the corner of my eye: Abel. Cursed or not, at that moment I was with my brother. Although he was departed and my heart was broken, I knew he was all right. There was a heaven; the proof had stood before me. And even though I would never see him again, it comforted me to know that he had been there. I thought to myself that if anyone knew my sorrow, it was he. I went to the barn and grabbed a shovel to bury my brother.

I dug for hours and never tired. By sundown the grave was dug, and I just sat with my brother at my side, my feet dangling in the fresh hole. I watched the sunset with him for the last time.

As the sun made its final reach for the horizon, I laid Abel and Powder to rest. I put the fresh soil atop their lifeless bodies. I planted roses, the most beautiful that anyone's ever seen, enough to cover the whole hill when they seasoned. I tore the altar down and proceeded to clean the entire farm, making it seem like this nightmare had never occurred. Then I left.

Chapter Five

The sun was starting to rise as I was walking away. I stopped and looked back. The farm was as black and lifeless as the path that lay before me. As I stood and watched the first rays of morning stretch across my former life, I turned my back to the sun and started off across the unknown.

I may not have been able to physically feel pain or even shed a tear, yet there were still many emotions present deep within my soul. I still had the memory of sadness and grief. I knew that getting as far as I could from that place was the right thing to do, yet the memory of fear made me want to stay. I just put it out of my mind and walked.

I walked for three straight days until I realized from the change of scenery that I had traveled a great distance. The surroundings were not barren like the lands that I once inhabited, where the only green was what we planted. This land was lush, and there were trees and animals unlike any that I had seen.

I calculated that it had been six days or more since anything had crossed my lips. I looked around for something that would pass for food. I found some berries growing wild in a wooded area. But as I put them to my lips, they turned to ash upon my tongue. I realized there was nothing that would satisfy my hunger.

Immediately, I looked for some water to cure my thirst. I walked again, this time for not so long. It seemed that I could cover long distances in a short period of time. When I was lost in thought and walking for three sundowns, I couldn't help but wonder how far that I had gone, not that it mattered much.

I could hear what sounded like a creek in the distance. I turned back and forth, trying to hone in on the sound, and tracked it to its source. The sound became louder as I got closer to my destination. It seemed that the creek would appear in front of me at any moment.

Finally, as I drew near, I realized how far off the creek really had been. It must have been two miles away when the sound first befell my ears. Anyhow, no matter how far off it had been, it didn't matter now because I was there.

The creek that I had found was deep and winding. The walls on either side were three men high, decorated with rocks and tall grasses. It was a beautiful sight, yet at the same time it was devastating. That spot will haunt me forever.

Imagine seeing the sun bathing trees and grasses that are bending to a glistening, stone-walled creek. The birds and animals here and there animate the scene right before your eyes. Now is when you can truly realize the cruelty of my punishment. I stood there as the branches of a nearby tree danced in the wind. I closed my eyes and smelled everything, but I could feel nothing: not the breeze upon my flesh nor the grass on my fingertips. I was dead to the world.

I decided to have a drink, so I approached the wall of the creek. Since the feeling in my legs was gone, I slipped, tumbling into the water. I stood there completely soaked and again felt nothing.

I tilted my head back to let the water drip into my mouth, but not a drop passed my lips. I stuck my head in the water to drink, but my throat closed off. I brought my head up and tried to force the water down my throat, but I could not swallow. I held the water in my mouth forever, it seemed, yet the result never changed. I opened my mouth, the water rushed out, and my mouth was left dry. Not only was there nothing to feed my hunger, there was also nothing to quench my thirst.

I climbed out of the creek and brushed myself off. Shifting my gaze to my leg, it came to my attention that a stick had found its way through my shin. I screamed and fell to the ground, grabbing at my leg. Then I realized that the usual pain was not there. It took me a while to get used to the vision of a stick poking out from both sides of my leg. I had to come to terms with the fact that I could not go on like that.

I slowly reached for the stick, gripping it firmly with both hands. I counted to three and yanked it out in one thrust. I went to scream, then realized there was no need: the pain was not there. As luck would have it, I couldn't see the wound through my rags. So I just threw the stick down and went on my way, although I was still unsure where my way was taking me. I figured that instead of wondering where I was going, I better just get somewhere.

That brought me to a cave. From a distance, it was beautiful. Carved into the side of a mountain, it had trees all around. Sunlight and dark greens and browns were perfectly draped upon the cold stone of the mountain. Inside the cave, it was dark and moist. My ears could pick up the slightest movements from the various things that called this cave their home.

All that mattered to me was that I could finally get far away from everyone. I could just sit and hide from the world. The sun tried to penetrate the darkness of my newfound home, but the concentrated darkness within snuffed it out at the massive, jagged opening. From inside, the opening resembled a gaping mouth with razor teeth emerging from the mountain above.

I walked deeper into the cave and turned to look upon the doorway again. The sun was starting to set. It was breathtaking, so I sat there in the middle of the cave and shut my eyes. Abel and Powder were still fresh in my mind. For a moment, it seemed that we were all perched upon our little hill. I could hear them in my head. Their smells lingered in my nostrils, as if I could open my eyes and they would be right next to me as they had always been.

Yet when I opened my eyes, the only thing to greet me was the darkness. I had spent so much time thinking of them that the sun had already sunk into the earth. The only light that remained was that of the faint moon overhead, tickling the opening. My mountain was sending an eerie feeling through me. I realized that my life would never be the same; this dismal cave was all I had.

I sat emotionless and stared out of the opening as if waiting for something to happen—like I knew something was going to happen. There was that unmistakable taste of fear that took over, sort of a metallic taste, and all my senses were heightened. Then, from the corner of my eye, I saw it: the shadow from the barn. It had to be. I would never forget that shadow, even though it was only briefly that I saw it. Some things that happen, even for an instant, stay with you longer and more vividly than things that you try to remember.

There it was again, further down the wall. It was going in and out of my vision like clouds in the moon's light, yet there was not a cloud in the sky. There was nothing to cut out a shadow. I thought for a moment that it was just another vivid memory flooding from my overworked brain. So I shook my head and closed my eyes again.

There was a long silence, which was odd because ever since I had stepped within these dark walls, there had been an orchestra of sound ricocheting through the dark. Then suddenly there was a snap, like someone breaking a twig right in my ear. My eyes flew open to reveal nothing. Nothing but the soft light of the moon.

Then again it was right beside me—the shadow, bold as ever it was, in a shade so black it didn't look real. It popped from the wall like it wasn't a shadow at all but a color-less entity. It moved with the wind. Pieces of black left the shadow like ash from a fire when the breeze blew through the cave.

The alarms inside my body were going off simultaneous-ly, creating a state of fear that I had never yet experienced. I turned, thinking that whatever was creating this shadow was right behind me. I turned, yet nothing was there.

Then I thought to look outside. I got up and cautiously made my way to the opening; again, nothing. As I turned to go back into the cave, there it stood, no longer hidden in shadow. I fell to the ground in fear. The last time I had encountered a winged entity, it had not gone well.

This one, unlike the one I had already encountered, was not white and golden with a glow from deep within its core. This one was tattered and black. All the different shades of black there could be were draped over this dark and crooked creature. He did not speak in my head as the other had. He actually spoke to me like he was an equal, even friendly in a way. Well, enough for the fear to disperse, anyway.

"Do not cower, Cain, for I am not here to harm you. I, too, am a castaway from heaven. I have fallen from grace and aimlessly roam the earth, just as you do."

I couldn't believe it. How could an angel be cast away? Yet I didn't care, for now it seemed that I was not alone.

"I am Lucifer. I once sat at the right hand of God himself. I was the first of the angels, the first created, in fact."

There was sincerity in his voice. A sadness was within him also.

Even so, a heightened sense awoke in me, as if something deep within me whispered caution. I tried not to make it obvious that I was getting insight and just looked upon him with confusion stretched across my face. "I'm sorry, there's just ... I mean, so much has happened to me that months ago seemed all but impossible. Yet here I am, punished by God through an angel over something that I didn't even know I did. Even now, I don't believe it. You would think that an all-knowing God would know I would never purposely harm my brother. I loved him. I mean, I love him. Even now that he is gone, I still love him. And now that he is in heaven with God, my brother will say that he loves me, too. That I would never purposely harm him. Then I will be forgiven. I just have to wait it out ... right?"

I don't know what came over me. Lucifer just seemed so comforting that I unloaded on him. It hurt getting that all out, and it started to anger me at the same time. It seemed cruel to let me keep all my emotions, but refuse me tears to cry to ease the pain. Or to bask in the warmth yet not feel the heat. Lost in thought and anger, I forgot that Lucifer was even there.

"There's nothing that you can do now. It is done. Once an angel bestows a gift or punishment, it is binding," Lucifer said. "The angels hold the power. That is our purpose: to watch, reward, and punish. God himself gave these powers to us, for he is creator of all and there is too much going on all over the world. This is just the beginning. Over time, the world will be overrun. And you, my friend, have slipped through the cracks."

There was a smile spreading across Lucifer's lips as he talked. I just sat there listening. For some time, he told me of the workings of heaven, the secrets and weaknesses of angels, and all the flaws and imperfections of God and the people made in his image. Feelings of jealousy unwillingly weaved themselves through his words.

Chapter Six

Lucifer fell silent, then he walked over to me and placed his hand on my shoulder. A window in my mind opened, and I witnessed firsthand the argument and punishment of Lucifer. You couldn't even tell it was him; in heaven, he had been beautiful. His magnificent wings were purple and flawless. Now they sat perched upon his back, tattered and black. Even his posture was crooked and frail. The fall from grace was horrifying to watch. It angered me to see the injustice that had been handed down to him.

Lucifer explained that in the beginning, there were thirteen angels, Lucifer being the highest. But they were flawed, for God gave them emotions. This was unlike his angels now, who acted without question like mindless pets. Lucifer turned and walked to the opening of the cave, looking to the heavens. "Even now they lack perfection, for they do not know what has just happened, do they?"

As he stood there in silence, his wings spread. The moon's rays found their way through the holes of his leathery wings, highlighting a single feather that still hung on. It verified the vision that we had shared moments earlier. He turned to me again. "What if I told you that I could alter some of the ailments that have been given to you? I cannot undo what has been done, but I can alter it to benefit you. I am still of a higher status than the new breed of angels." Lucifer put his hands together and started to rub them. "Well, what say you, do you wish to spread your wings?"

"My wings? What do you mean, and why do you need my permission?"

"For we who are still bound by ancient law, our help must be asked for."

"We?" I asked.

He motioned behind him, where stood the twelve that had

followed him to the abyss. "We are legion; we can bestow upon you great power. All you have to do is ask."

They waited, somewhat impatiently except for Lucifer. He was unmoving. I looked into his eyes; they gave no indication of haste. He had a way of making me feel comforted, like he wanted to help. There was sympathy when he looked upon me.

Then there was a change in his voice. A hint of malice tangled within his words. "Look at you. Look upon the man they created."

Lucifer spread his hands, one atop the other. A pool of water appeared, the fluid spinning between his hands. Instantly the fluid froze and lit up with a faint red light. He held his hands in front of me, and for the first time I realized what had been done to me. My face was misshapen and scorched. Lifting my hands to my face, I noticed the mark of God burned into both of my hands: the mark of a murderer, put where everyone could see. The mark was burned clear through so that the image was visible on both sides of my hands.

Then the makeshift mirror showed Ariel bestowing my punishment, a faint smile stretching across his face as I was tortured. I watched my body fly over the hill, and Ariel's face again as he brought my body to me. "How could this be an angel of God?" I thought.

"Look at how he stripped you of everything, for a mistake. Where is the love, where is the forgiveness that a shepherd is supposed to show his flock? Instead, he sends his mindless sheep do his bidding, not knowing that his sheep have yet again found emotion." Lucifer froze the image of Ariel. "Look into his eyes. Look at what happened, just as I told him it would. It is his folly that did this to you."

"I don't understand," I said. There was obviously more going on than I knew.

"We, the first thirteen, were given emotions." He moved his hands and the mirror dispersed. Lucifer looked into my eyes again, then waved his hand. A stone rose from the ground before me. He sat in front of me, calmly speaking. "That is why I was cast out. We were given all the emotions of the people that now inhabit this world, including free will, which caused us to question and act out, so to speak. God did not approve; he did not like that we questioned him or went against his punishments. We felt remorse for the lesser beings. We had to do unspeakable things during our time in heaven.

"You humans were not the first race to inhabit this world. First, there were giant beasts that walked the earth. When they got out of hand, we wiped them out, killing every species there was. This was hard for us to do. We fought this decision, and that's when we were banished. Then, a thousand years later, I saw a new breed of angels. They were scouting the world for any remains of the lives we had destroyed. I followed them, keeping to the shadows. They were different, moving as if they had no minds of their own."

The look on Lucifer's face went almost blank as he went back in his mind. I felt that I wasn't even there anymore. It was quite obvious that he had never told anyone his story before. In fact, it seemed that he was glad to finally get it off his chest.

Then he continued, "I followed this new breed for some time. Then they found them," Lucifer stated. "As an attempt to right our wrongs, we had revived some small creatures, thinking that they would go undetected. They did for some time." He tightened his fist. "Until, that is, the angels found them. They wiped the animals out with no hesitation.

"Over time, I started to notice a change in these angels. Their eyes started to change. Just as I knew they would, they were gaining emotion. But above all, it was jealousy that I noticed. I had foreseen a time when this would happen."

Lucifer motioned to me. "You, my child, are a result of faulty design, a mistake of God, and you, like me, are wiped from the book. But to his surprise, you will not be wiped so easily. So what say you?" He held the mirror to me again. This time he showed me a more beautiful reflection, almost flawless, with shadows behind me that resembled wings. "Will you join me? All you need to do is ask, and all you see will be yours."

I studied the vision before me. Reluctantly, I said, "Will you help me? Will you bestow on me this vision that I see before me? Please."

With that, Lucifer smiled and replied, "So let it be done." He clapped his hands together. The sound was deafening as it echoed through the cave, bouncing off the walls to the depths of the mountain.

"Is that it, what happened ?" I asked.

"Yesss, that's it," Lucifer hissed as he stood before me. I raised my hands; the marks were still there. "I said that I can only alter what has been done. You will always bear those marks, I'm afraid. They will always be a reminder of that day. Let them feed your wrath."

And they did. There was now a difference about me. There was anger and resentment bubbling up inside me. "Let me see what you have done, Lucifer. Let me see my face."

Lucifer created his mirror again and beckoned me into the moonlight. I couldn't believe it—I had the beauty of an angel. I went to touch my face, and I could feel. Not completely, though; it was dulled from what I remembered, but it still felt good to touch again.

Then my glance was interrupted. The moon highlighted my eyes, and they were black, completely black. It startled me. They were beautiful and frightening at the same time. "What happened to my eyes?"

As I spoke, I noticed my teeth. They were whiter than any that I had seen. Their appearance was remarkable; I was in awe. I opened my mouth. "My teeth, they are those of a beast, fanged and sharp!"

"All I have done is help you. It was not my doing to curse you to drink only blood or eat of nothing but ash. That cannot be undone, either. Can you imagine trying to drink blood with nothing to break the skin? This way, you are equipped with speed to do the unthinkable. Haste will shorten the pain of your memories every time you try."

Lucifer then started to walk around me. "The angels made it impossible for you to die, wanting you to suffer for eternity. Now you and I can make them suffer for their follies. Neither man nor beast, angel nor God can undo what has been done. It will be their fatal mistake."

With that, Lucifer pulled his robes up his arm, extending his wrist in front of my face and asking me to drink of his vein. "Another difference from the angels of times forgotten. Drink and take the final step. Drink and leave the world in ash."

I put his wrist to my mouth and let my new fangs find their way through his angelic flesh. Then, as if it were even a surprise to him, I grabbed his arm and drank deep. He had to pry away from my grasp, ripping my teeth from his perfect arm. The blood within his veins was golden in color and tasted like heaven. I could not control myself.

The look Lucifer gave me at that moment told me he had instantly realized he had made a mistake. He put his hand over his arm. I could smell his fluid leaving his torn flesh. He looked as if he was trying to heal himself, but had trouble succeeding. "The final transformation is complete," he stated. Then he stepped backwards into the shadows and disappeared.

Watching Lucifer sink back into the cave wall, all I could think about was chasing him down. The blood of an angel was still dripping from my chin. The feeling was indescribable, yet as I lunged into the shadow, the hard stone of the mountain was all there was left. He had vanished.

Violent thoughts raced through my head. I fell to the floor of the cave, my head in my hands. There were visions of death flooding through my thoughts, things I'd never seen before. They were visions of violence yet to come, whole villages falling to my unquenchable thirst. Lucifer's blood was slowly working its way through my system. I could faintly feel the warmth in my body. The sweet poison now inhabited my body, slowly driving me insane.